Other Cecil Aldin titles published by Souvenir Press

A Dog Day
Sleeping Partners

For Katy and Dominic

Puppy Dogs' Tales

Pictured by
Cecil Aldin

Told by
Roy Heron

Souvenir Press

Cecil Aldin illustrations
© Anthony C. Mason

Text © Roy Heron 2002

First published 2002 by
Souvenir Press Ltd.,
43 Great Russell Street,
London WCI B 3PD

ISBN 028563656 1

Typeset by Dorchester Typesetting,
Dorchester
Colour reproduction by Colourscript,
Mildenhall
Printed in Italy

Contents

Introduction

When Cecil Aldin died in 1935, the *Daily Mirror* proclaimed in a front-page tribute that he had "achieved world fame by his delightful dog studies" and *The Times* went further, stating "there never yet has been a painter of dogs fit to hold a candle to him". The verdict was echoed on both sides of the Atlantic by writers and broadcasters who recalled the wonderful canine portraits he produced in the last decade of his life. But he first achieved fame before the 1914-18 war and the illustrations for this book have been selected from a series first published in that period. The Great War, as it was called, was a watershed in his life as it was for so many others. In the decade before the war he produced a veritable avalanche of canine drawings for the juvenile market and the inspiration for them was provided by his two children, Dudley and Gwen. Some of the first of his comical dogs were painted on the walls of their nursery, in the form of a chase, and, as the children demanded more, the drawings grew into a frieze that encircled the room. He joined forces with his friend John Hassall and the frieze was turned into decorative panels, which were sold through a wallpaper manufacturer. The Queen of Spain bought a set and some can still be seen in the nurseries of British stately homes, such as those preserved by the National Trust.

The drawings are all based on animals Aldin knew. When he was working on them his household included thirteen dogs, two horses, a donkey, a parrot and two monkeys, to say nothing of the casual visitors. Over the years he built up a reference library of dog sketches from life, which eventually comprised more than two thousand drawings and which he referred to constantly. Anyone who has owned, or had a close association with a dog will recognise the characteristics. No-one captured the essence of dogdom better than Aldin and people would often refer to "a Cecil Aldin dog" they had seen.

His first venture into this field was a slim volume called *A Dog Day*, which became the most popular dog book in the world and has been in print, almost continuously, for a hundred years. Such is the quality of these books that they are treasured by parents and children alike and they are now much sought-after by collectors. As for the subjects of the stories, it will be noticed that frolics and food play a major role. The dogs always seem to be on the look-out for mischief, usually with a purloined snack in mind. Food, of course, is the prime motivation of a puppy's life. I had a young Labrador who one afternoon ate the heels off a brand new pair of shoes, followed by a dozen fresh eggs taken from a shopping basket, including the shells, and half the legs of a chair (it was soft wood). On another occasion, when left in the kitchen, he disposed of a sizeable leg of lamb, bone and all. The pair of terriers who live with me at present are fairly well behaved when left in the house, but forage voraciously in the garden and fields, sampling anything from flower heads and meadow grass to worm casts and rabbit droppings. Here I should stress that none of my dogs has lacked "normal" food.

The most important attribute Aldin looked for in a dog was character and none had more of that elusive quality than Tatters, a little wire-haired terrier, who was a self-feeder. At the time, Aldin was working on a book about ancient buildings and he travelled in an open top car, which he found useful because he could park in the road and draw to his heart's content while still sitting in the driver's seat, Always on these trips, lasting for several days, his sole companion was Tatters. Whenever Aldin stopped in a town or village, Tatters jumped out and went in search of a food shop. If the shop door was closed, Tatters waited patiently for a customer to open it. Then he would sit up and beg in the centre of the shop, waving his paws in the air and with a pleading look on his face, until someone took pity and threw him a morsel of food. It was the performance of a consummate professional beggar and Tatters repeated it until he had had his fill. If Tatters was not in sight when Aldin was ready to leave, a toot on the car horn was enough to bring him scurrying from his latest eating place.

Aldin's first "professional" dog model was Gyp, a smooth-haired fox terrier, who would hold a pose for fifteen minutes in exchange for a biscuit. Sometimes Aldin used his friends' dogs. One such was a Sealyham called Slickson, who was in the same league as Tatters when it came to begging Slickson had very short legs, a tubby body and a stump of a tail, proportions which were perfect for balancing in the required position. This ability made Slickson useful to the artist and the Sealyham was featured three tines in a Christmas coloured plate which

Aldin produced for the *Illustrated London News*. Another Sealyham terrier, Susan, was among the last dogs owned by Aldin and went with him to Majorca, his final "place in the sun". Susan was an inveterate hunter, but her other claim to fame was being a guide to a blind Irish wolfhound, who stayed with Aldin to have his portrait painted. In unfamiliar surroundings, the blind dog blundered into furniture, until Susan took a hand. For the rest of his stay, the giant wolfhound followed the tiny Sealyham everywhere, being guided by scent and touch.

Much of the fun had gone out of Aldin's life with the onset of war in 1914. He became a Remount officer, finding horses for the Army. His daughter helped in the stables and his only son joined the Royal Engineers. Dudley was killed, aged 19, at Vimy Ridge and Aldin never fully recovered from the blow. After the war he turned to more serious subjects and it was not until his grandchildren, Tony and Ann, were born that much of his *joie de vivre* was restored. During holidays with the children on Exmoor he organised the first mongrel dog shows, an idea that has been widely copied. There were prizes for such classes as The Dog With the Bandiest Legs and The Dog With the Most Sympathetic Eyes. Three dogs owned by Mrs (later Lady) A. J. Munnings were jointly adjudged the worst mongrels, but by no means all of the entrants were mongrels. A prize for The Ugliest Dog in Show went to the artist's favourite model, Cracker the bull terrier.

SCAMP'S TALE

I'm Scamp by name and scamp by
   nature
Always out for a big adventure

This is Rex, who thinks himself a
  beauty
A real pedigree little Lord Snooty

Here comes Chumpy, no
  thoroughbred he.
Now we'll have fun with Rex, just
  you see

We urge and cajole him to join our
game.
Rex looks straight through us and
sniffs in disdain

High tea and low plates, too much a
temptation.
Chump's first, by a length, to my
aggravation

Rex leaves in a carriage, a smile on
  his face.
We finish our cake and decide to
  give chase

Oh, what a fine wheeze, to scatter
the sheep.
I know it's wrong, but my
conscience will keep

The farmer's so angry I fear for my
   life,
So I'll dig myself in and hide from
   the strife

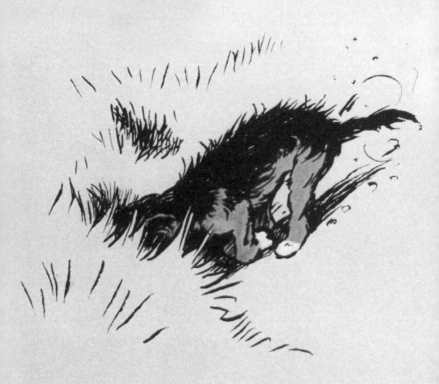

"You're covered in mud," the
   gardener said
And poured cold water all over my
   head

Into the house I run, wet through
    and through
And find some clean towels – well,
    wouldn't you?

I'm stood in a corner, "A really bad
  boy,"
Yet I've no regrets for a day full of
  joy

BOBTAIL BILL'S TALE

I'm bob-tailed Bill, because I've
  none to wag.
Tim laughs, but his tail leaves no
  room to brag

Another tail-wagger, not my brother.
He's scoffing at my lack of a rudder

Down to the pond, I drink 'till I'm
 sated
While ducks chuckle for reasons
 just stated

Even the calf has time to despise
My lack of a swish to ward off the
 flies

Worse still, a nanny goat bleats with
  glee
At poor, embarrassed, blunt-ended
  me

Surely the lamb will be my friend. "Baa," he says. "You've a baa-re rear end"

I know this white terrier will not
  mock.
I'm wrong. He, too, sneers at my
  dry dock

It must really be the final straw
When a cat laughs as I pass her door

At last I've found how I can fool 'em.
I'll squat, and thus keep my decorum

SNOWBALL'S TALE

They call me Snowball, a likeable pup,
Pestered by cats, whose milk I will
sup

I thought I'd give the two kittens a
  fright
Then, just like lightning, they
  scratch and they bite

Nipper's my cousin, a bow-tied
  young bore
And these soppy pups live with him,
  next door

Here's Snap, and that look, what
   does it portend?
Sure to be mischief with food at the
   end

I'm feeling hungry, with no snack in
   sight,
Trying in vain to catch this bird in
   flight

I've drunk the cat's milk and she's
   quite upset,
Not that I'm worried by that feline pet

Our neighbour's thrown this well-
    aimed boot
Because I acquired his chops – the
    brute!

The cats left their cream – I drank it
down quick.
It must have been sour, for now I
feel sick.

I'm deep in disgrace for stealing the
    meat.
Except for the cream, it went down a
    treat

POPPY'S TALE

They call me Poppy because I'm red.
This dolly's cradle makes a fine bed

The children's toys are dull as a
   carrot.
Not so much fun as a real live
   parrot

Shiver me timbers, I've upset his cage
And pretty Polly's in a fine old rage

I've explored some more and found
   a rabbit
Who flaps both his ears, an awful
   habit

Are these ears really real, I wonder,
And try to wrench this one asunder

More fun, an unattended can of
   paint.
The taste and smell make this young
   dog feel faint

Oh, crumbs! The upturned can gave
   me a fright
And I've became a Poppy red and
   white

Here's a convenient door to wipe my
   back on.
Who knows? This stripey look may
   start a fashion

My owner's skirt is next for my
  devotion,
But when she sees the paint, what a
  commotion!

The paint has gone, and so has my
  good name.
I'm exiled, chained and kennelled
  for my crime